Can You Guess My Name?

Can You Guess My Name?

TRADITIONAL TALES AROUND THE WORLD

SELECTED AND RETOLD BY Judy Sierra

ILLUSTRATED BY Stefano Vitale

Clarion Books • New York

Clarion Books
a Houghton Mifflin Company imprint
215 Park Avenue South, New York, NY 10003

The illustrations were executed in oil paint on mixed surfaces and collage.
The text was set in 13-point Cochin.

www.houghtonmifflinbooks.com

Printed in Singapore.

Library of Congress Cataloging-in-Publication Data

Sierra, Judy.
Can you guess my name? : traditional tales around the world /
[selected and retold] by Judy Sierra ; illustrated by Stefano Vitale.
p. cm.
Summary: A collection of fifteen folktales from all over the world, including stories that resemble
"The Three Pigs," "The Bremen Town Musicians," and "Rumpelstiltskin."
Includes bibliographical references.
ISBN 0-618-13328-3
1. Tales. [1. Folklore.] I. Vitale, Stefano, ill. II. Title.
PZ8.1.S573 Can 2002   398.2—dc21   2002003509

TWP 10 9 8 7 6 5 4 3 2 1

To my uncle and aunt,
John and Jeannette Law
—J.S.

To my tribe
—S.V.

CONTENTS

I MARRIED A FROG

THE SCARY HOUSE IN THE BIG WOODS

INTRODUCTION

Many of the world's folktales resemble one another in surprising ways, as anyone who hears them or reads them soon discovers. Familiar characters and episodes and even similar plots appear in tales from many cultures. How did this happen? The world's oral tales probably spread and gradually changed over a long period of time, in the course of humankind's migrations, trade, and exploration. Folklorists have tried to trace the history of specific kinds of tales—Cinderella tales, for instance—but even though they examined hundreds of different versions, no one has been able to explain where any folktale originated or how it spread. There is just not enough evidence.

Why certain folktales have such enduring appeal is an easier question to answer. They are remembered and shared because they explore timeless human concerns in exciting, entertaining ways. For example, tales for children and adolescents, like those in this collection, seek to answer such questions as: If an evil monster kidnapped me, could I escape? When I leave home, will I be able to survive on my own? Will I marry the right person?

The fifteen tales I selected for this collection resemble five European folktale classics: "The Three Pigs," "The Bremen Town Musicians," "Rumpelstiltskin," "The Frog Prince," and "Hansel and Gretel." Some of these tales I found polished to near-perfection in old books and journals, like "Three Little Piggies and Old Mister Fox," published a century ago in *The Journal of American Folklore*. I retold others, like "Medio Pollito" and "Oniroku," from several different sources.

In scholarly folklore collections, tale texts are often incomplete or bare-bones versions. When one of these has the potential to become a good story, I retell it by combining different versions and adding details like words, refrains, and dialogue from similar tales, songs, riddles, and proverbs of the same culture. Finally, I tell my works-in-progress to groups of children, and their responses help me fine-tune the tales.

Parents and teachers can use the tales in this book to introduce children to comparative literature (in many countries, folktales are the only published literature for children). Children enjoy discussing the similarities and differences among tales. Environmental details—types of animals, food, houses, etc.—often differ from culture to culture, while the messages of the tales (at least of the tales in this book) are similar. By looking at who is rewarded and who is punished, for example, children can see what sorts of behaviors are considered good and bad across cultures.

I hope you will enjoy these stories as much as I have.

I'LL BLOW YOUR HOUSE IN!

Tales like "The Three Pigs"

The story of three little pigs and a big bad wolf is one of the best-known folktales of the English-speaking world. Many versions from the oral tradition, like the following Scottish-American tale, "The Three Little Piggies and Old Mister Fox," recount the third pig's adventures after the wolf's failure to blow down the house. The little piggy proves that he or she is a bold trickster who can keep the wolf away from the door as well as escape, outwit, and humiliate him in the wider world. Until recently, tales like "The Three Pigs" were not known outside Europe and former European colonies. The idea of moving far from home and living on one's own, as characters do in these tales, was once unthinkable in most parts of the world.

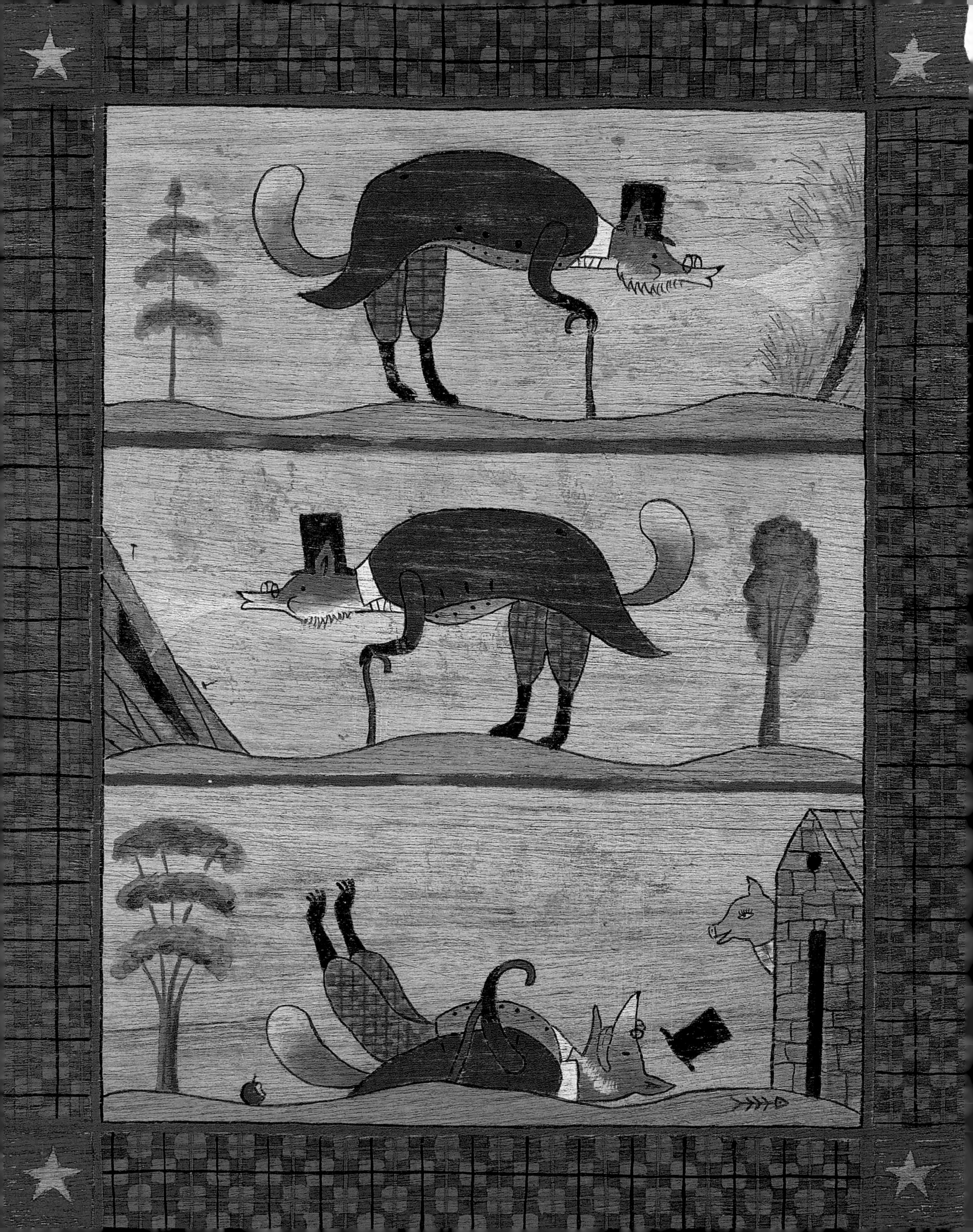

THE THREE LITTLE PIGGIES AND OLD MISTER FOX

United States: Scottish American

Once there was an old sow who had three little pigs. The first little piggy asked, "Mother, may I go out and seek my fortune?"

"No, no, because if you do, Old Mister Fox will eat you ALL UP."

"He won't be able to catch me if you build me a house of straw."

So the old sow built her first little piggy a house of straw.

Then along came Old Mister Fox and said, "Piggy, Piggy, please let me in."

But Piggy would not.

"Then I'll go up on top of your house, and blow and blow, and knock it down, and eat you ALL UP!"

Piggy would not let him in.

So Old Mister Fox went up on top of the house, and blew and blew, and knocked it down, and ate Piggy ALL UP.

Then the second little pig asked, "Mother, may I go out and seek my fortune?"

"No, no. Old Mister Fox will eat you ALL UP, just like he did your little brother."

"No, he won't—not if you build me a house of wood."

So the old sow built her second little piggy a house of wood.

Along came Old Mister Fox and said, "Piggy, Piggy, please let me in."

But Piggy would not.

"If you don't, I'll go up on top of your house, and blow and blow, and knock it down, and eat you ALL UP!"

Piggy would not let him in.

So Old Mister Fox went up on top of the house, and blew and blew, and knocked it down, and ate poor Piggy ALL UP.

Then the third little pig asked," Mother, may I go out and seek my fortune?"

"No, no. Old Mister Fox will eat you ALL UP, as he did your little brothers."

"No, he won't—not if you build me a house of stone."

So the old sow built her third little piggy a house of stone.

Then along came Old Mister Fox and said, "Piggy, Piggy, please let me in."

But Piggy would not.

"If you don't, I'll go up on top of your house, and blow and blow, and knock it down, and eat you ALL UP."

Piggy would not let him in.

So Old Mister Fox went up on top of the house, and blew and blew till he blew his whistle off. But he couldn't make that house budge. Old Mister Fox climbed down and said, "Piggy, Piggy, don't you want some nice apples?"

Piggy said, "Yes, I do."

"Well! Come over to my house in the morning, and I'll give you ALL you can pack home."

So Piggy went *really* early in the morning, before Mister Fox was up, and took all Mister Fox's apples, and took 'em home, and peeled 'em. She threw the peelings out the door, and she was just turning the key in the lock as Old Mister Fox came along.

"Piggy, Piggy, where did you get such nice apples?"

"I went over to your house before you were up and took ALL you had."

"Piggy, Piggy, don't you want some nice potatoes? Come over to my house in the morning, and I'll give you ALL you can pack home."

So Piggy went over *really* early the next morning, before Mister Fox got up, and took ALL he had, and carried 'em home, and peeled 'em, and threw the peelings out the door. She was just turning the key in the lock as Old Mister Fox came along.

"Piggy, Piggy, where did you get such nice potatoes?"

"I went over to your house before you were up and took ALL you had."

"Piggy, Piggy, don't you want some nice fish?"

Piggy said, "Yes, I do."

"Well! Come over to my house in the morning, and I'll give you ALL you can pack home."

So Piggy went over *really* early in the morning, before Mister Fox was up, and took ALL he had, and took 'em home, and scaled 'em, and threw the scales out the door. She was just turning the key in the lock as Old Mister Fox came along.

"Piggy, Piggy, where did you get such nice fish?"

"Why, I went down to the river and held my tail in the water all night, and when the fish nibbled, I pulled them up."

"Do you think I could catch any with *my* tail?"

"Yes, you could," said Piggy.

So Old Mister Fox went down to the river and held his tail in the water ALL night, and in the morning it was frozen fast, and he *couldn't* get it out.

By and by Piggy came down to the river with her kettle to get water to make her coffee, and there sat Old Mister Fox, his tail frozen in the ice, fast and tight.

"Piggy, Piggy, please chop me out."

"No, no; you'd eat me ALL UP."

"No, no, Piggy. I won't, I promise."

So she went back to the house, and got her hatchet, and chopped and chopped till she got Mister Fox's tail out of the ice, and he GRABBED her.

"Now—I've—got—you!—Now—I'll—eat—you—ALL—UP!" cried Old Mister Fox.

But Piggy slipped away, and she ran and ran, and got in her house, and slammed the door, and put her back against it just as Old Mister Fox came up.

"Piggy, Piggy, please let me put my nose in your house. I'm so cold."

So she let him put his nose in.

"Oh, Piggy! It smells so nice in here. Please let me put my eyes in your house."

So she let him put his eyes in.

"Oh, Piggy! It looks so beautiful in here. Please let me put my ears in."

So she let him put his ears in.

"Oh, Piggy! The kettle sounds so nice. Please let me put my whole head in."

So she let him put his whole head in.

"Oh, Piggy! My head's so nice and warm. Please let my front legs in."

So she let him put his front legs in.

"Oh, Piggy! My front legs are so good and warm. Please let me put my body in."

So she let him put his body in.

Then he JUMPED, and his hind legs and tail came in.

"Now—I've—got—you!—Now—I'll—eat—you—ALL—UP!" cried Old Mister Fox.

But Piggy said, "Oh, dear! What's that I hear? It sounds like a pack of hounds coming!"

"Oh, Piggy! Where can I hide? Where can I hide?" cried Old Mister Fox.

"Just jump into my butter churn."

So Old Mister Fox jumped into Piggy's butter churn, and Piggy took the kettle of boiling water and poured it over him, and then she churned, and she churned, and she churned till she churned Mister Fox ALL to butter!

BIG PIG, LITTLE PIG, SPECKLED PIG, AND RUNT

United States: African American

One time, way back yonder, there was an old widow sow with four children named Big Pig, Little Pig, Speckled Pig, and Runt. One day, the mama sow knew she was going to kick the bucket, so she took and called up all her children and told them that the time had come when they would have to look out for themselves. Then she up and told them, as well as she could, though brief and mighty scant, about what a bad creature old Br'er Wolf was. She said that if they could make their escape from old Br'er Wolf, they'd be doing monstrously well for themselves.

Big Pig bragged that she wasn't scared, and Little Pig allowed as she wasn't scared, either, and Speckled Pig said he was nearly as big as Br'er Wolf himself. Little Runt just rolled around and rooted in the straw while their mama went on telling them how mean and deceitful Br'er Wolf was.

Not long after that, sure enough, the sow lay down and died, and all her children were on their own, and they set about to build houses to live in.

Big Pig, she took and built herself a house out of brush, and Little Pig, she built a stick house. Speckled Pig, he built a mud house. Runt, without any great to-do, no bragging, went to work and built a rock house.

By and by, when they were all fixed in their houses, here comes Br'er Wolf, licking his chops and shaking his tail. First house he came to was Big Pig's house. Br'er Wolf walked up to the door and knocked sort of soft—*blim! blim! blim!* This woke Big Pig, and she came to the door and asked, "Who's that?"

Br'er Wolf allowed as how it was a friend, and he sang out,

"If you open the door and let me in,
I'll just warm my paws and go home again."

Still Big Pig asked, "Who's that?" and then Br'er Wolf, he up and asks, "How's your mama?"

"My mama died," says Big Pig, "and before she died, she told me, 'Be sure to keep your eye on Br'er Wolf.' I can see you through the crack of the door, and you look mighty like Br'er Wolf."

Then old Br'er Wolf drew a long breath and said, "I don't know how your ma could say that about me. Must have been her sickness and all. I came because I heard she was sick and I thought I'd drop by and bring her this bag of corn. I know if your ma were here right now, she'd take these roasting ears and be glad to get 'em. More than that, she'd invite me in by the fire to warm my paws."

All that talk about roasting ears made Big Pig's mouth water, and she opened the door and let Br'er Wolf inside, but before she had time to even let out a squeal, Br'er Wolf gobbled her up.

Next day, old Br'er Wolf played the same game with Little Pig. He sang his song and Little Pig let him inside, and he opened his mouth and let Little Pig inside.

Then Br'er Wolf paid a call on Speckled Pig, and he rapped at the door and sang,

"If you open the door and let me in,
I'll just warm my paws and go home again."

Speckled Pig suspected something, so he refused to open the door. But Br'er Wolf talked mighty soft and he talked mighty sweet. By and by he pushed his nose in the crack of the door, and he asked Speckled Pig if he could just put one paw inside and said he wouldn't go any further. He got that paw in, and then he begged to get the other paw in, and then his head. Then Br'er Wolf shoved the door open and ate up Speckled Pig.

The next day, Br'er Wolf thought he might as well eat Runt, too. Runt was the smallest, but word had gotten around that she was as smart as if she was full-grown, so Br'er Wolf knew he'd have to trick her good.

Br'er Wolf crept up to Runt's house and knocked at her door—*blam! blam! blam!*

"Who's that?" asked Runt.

"It's Big Pig," said Br'er Wolf. "I fetched you some sweet corn for your supper."

Runt looked through the crack of the door, and she laughed. "Big Pig never had that much hair on her hoof," she said.

Then old Br'er Wolf, he got mad. He decided to go down the chimney. But Runt heard a noise on the wall and guessed what was happening. She took a pile of broom sage, and when she heard Br'er Wolf walking across the roof to the chimney, she got the fire tongs and shoved the broom straw on the fire. The smoke made Br'er Wolf's head swim, and he dropped down, and before he knew it, he was burnt to a crackling. That was the last of old Br'er Wolf. Leastwise, it was the end of *that* Br'er Wolf!

THE THREE GEESE

Italy

Once upon a time, there lived three geese who were greatly afraid of the wolf, for they knew that if he found them, he would eat them. One day, the eldest goose said to her two sisters, "Do you know what I think? I think that if we build a little house, the wolf won't be able to catch us and eat us. Shall we go and look for something to build a house with?"

"Yes, yes," said her sisters, and off they flapped until they found a man who had a load of straw. "Good fellow," said the geese, "please give us a little of that straw to make a house, so that the wolf won't eat us."

"Take it, take it!" the man said, and he gave them as much straw as they could carry. The geese thanked the man, and they carried the straw to a meadow, where they built a lovely little house with a kitchen and not one but *two* balconies—everything a goose could possibly want.

When the house was finished, the eldest goose went inside.

Quickly, she locked the door with a padlock. Then she wandered out on the balcony and called down to her sisters, "I shall be very comfortable here *alone*. Go away, for I want nothing to do with either of you."

The two little geese began to cry. They begged their sister to open the door and let them in, for if she did not, the wolf would surely find them and eat them. But their sister would not listen, and so the two little ones went on their way. At last they met a man who had a load of sticks, and they said to him, "Kind sir, please give us some of those sticks to build a house, so that the wolf will not find us and eat us!"

"Yes, yes. Take all you want," said the man, and he gave them as many sticks as they could carry. The geese were so pleased! They thanked the man, and carried the sticks to another meadow, and built a pretty little house, much prettier than the first.

The middle-sized goose said to the smallest, "Listen. I am going inside now to see whether I am comfortable in this house." Once she was inside, the goose said to herself, "I like this house so much, I don't want to share it with my sister. I shall be very happy here alone." She fastened the door with a padlock, and went out on the balcony, and called down to her sister, "This is such a cozy house. I don't want you here! Go away and leave me alone."

The smallest goose began to weep. She begged her sister to let her in, for she was alone and did not know where to go, and if the wolf found her, he would eat her. But it did no good. Her cruel sister shut the balcony door.

Then the little goose traveled on alone, and at last she met a man who had a load of iron and stones. "Good man," said the goose, "please give me some of those stones and a little of that iron to build a house, so that the wolf won't find me and eat me!"

"Yes, yes, little goose," said the man. "Take some, and I will help you build your house." Then they found another meadow and built a pretty house, with *three* balconies, and a garden all around. The house was very strong, for it was lined with iron, and the doors were iron also. The little goose thanked the man and went inside.

Now let us go to the wolf. All this time, he had been looking everywhere for the three geese but could not find them. Then he learned that they had built three houses, and he searched until he came to the meadow where the first house stood. He knocked at the door.

"Who is there?" asked the biggest goose.

"A good friend," said the wolf. "Open the door and let me in."

"No, no," said the goose. "You sound like the wolf, and I will not open the door, because you will eat me."

"Open up, I say. Don't be afraid."

"No, no!" squawked the goose.

"Very well, then," said the wolf, "I will blow down your little straw house." And indeed, he blew down the house in one breath, and ate up the goose. "Now that I have eaten one," he said, "I absolutely must eat the other two."

The wolf searched until he found the house of the second

goose, and everything happened as before. The wolf blew down the house and ate the goose. Then he went in search of the littlest goose, and when he found her house, he knocked at the door, but she would not let him in. Then he tried to blow the house down, but of course he couldn't, because it was built of iron and stones. Then the wolf climbed on the roof and jumped up and down, but he only hurt his feet and broke his toenails. He growled and muttered, "One way or another I *will* eat you."

The wolf came down from the roof and went to the door of the house and said, "Dear goose, shall we be friends? You are such a nice little goose. Why don't we get together tomorrow and cook some macaroni? You can make the pasta, and I will bring the butter and cheese."

"Why, that's a splendid idea," said the little goose. "Come at noon with the butter and cheese."

The next day, the little goose got up early and went to town and bought some flour, and carried it home, and set about making pasta. A little before noon, the wolf arrived and knocked at the door and said, "Come, Goosey, open the door, for I have brought you the butter and cheese!"

The goose went up to her balcony and said, "Pass them up to me."

So the wolf lifted the butter and cheese up to the goose, who said, "Go take a walk while I finish cooking, and come back at two o'clock." She put a big kettle full of water on the fire, and soon it was boiling.

At two o'clock, the wolf returned. "Come, Goosey dear, open the door," he cried.

"No, I will not open it," said the little goose, "for when I am cooking I don't want anyone in the way. After the macaroni is done, I will open the door, and you may come in and eat it."

So the wolf waited and waited, and he grew hungrier and hungrier. A little while later, the goose said, "Would you like to try a bit of macaroni to see whether it is well cooked?"

"Open the door and let me taste it," begged the wolf.

"No, no. You can't come in yet. Put your lips on the keyhole and I will pour the macaroni into your mouth."

The wolf, all greedy as he was, put his mouth to the keyhole. The little goose lifted the kettle to the door and poured boiling water through the keyhole, and the wolf was scalded and killed. Then the little goose took a knife and cut open the wolf's stomach, and out jumped her two sisters, who were still alive, for the wolf had swallowed them whole. The two sisters begged the little goose's pardon for the mean way they had treated her, and the little goose, because she was kindhearted, forgave them and took them into her house, and there they ate macaroni and lived happily.

JUST THE RIGHT FRIENDS

Tales like "The Bremen Town Musicians"

The three tales that follow are part a group of "nursery quest tales" in which unpromising heroes and heroines—small ones like Master Thumb, and ill-formed ones like Medio Pollito—leave home and defeat a powerful opponent. As they go forth, these minuscule adventurers just happen to meet helpful animals and acquire magic objects that will prove essential to their success. If, for example, the hero befriends a cat, we can expect that scratching or meowing will be called for later on. If a flood occurs, the lucky hero will just happen to have a boat in his pocket. Animals and objects in these tales not only walk and talk, they often conveniently shrink and grow, so that the hero can carry them. These tales demonstrate the old adage "It isn't what you know, it's who you know."

HOW JACK WENT TO SEEK HIS FORTUNE

United States: Anglo-American

Once upon a time, there was a boy named Jack who went to seek his fortune. Jack hadn't gone very far when he met a cat.

"Where are you going, Jack?" asked the cat.

"I am going to seek my fortune," Jack answered.

"May I go with you?" asked the cat.

"Yes," said Jack. "The more the merrier."

So on they went, *jiggelty-jolt, jigglety-jolt,* and by and by they met a dog.

"Where are you going, Jack?" asked the dog.

"I am going to seek my fortune," Jack answered.

"May I go with you?" asked the dog.

"Yes," said Jack. "The more the merrier."

So on they went, *jiggelty-jolt, jigglety-jolt,* and by and by they met a goat.

"Where are you going, Jack?" asked the goat.

"I am going to seek my fortune," Jack answered.

"May I go with you?" asked the goat.

"Yes," said Jack. "The more the merrier."

So on they went, *jigglety-jolt, jigglety-jolt,* and by and by they met a bull.

"Where are you going, Jack?" asked the bull.

"I am going to seek my fortune," Jack answered.

"May I go with you?" asked the bull.

"Yes," said Jack. "The more the merrier."

So on they went, *jigglety-jolt, jigglety-jolt,* and by and by they met a rooster.

"Where are you going, Jack?" asked the rooster.

"I am going to seek my fortune," Jack answered.

"May I go with you?" asked the rooster.

"Yes," said Jack. "The more the merrier."

So on they went, *jigglety-jolt, jigglety-jolt,* until it was about dark, and they began to wonder where they would spend the night.

Around this time they came in sight of a house, and Jack told the animals to keep still while he went up and looked through the window. What did Jack see? Inside the house, a band of mean, ugly robbers were counting their money!

Jack went back to where the animals were and whispered, "Wait till I give the word, and then make all the noise you can."

When they were all ready, Jack gave the word. The cat mewed, and the dog barked, and the goat blatted, and the bull bellowed, and the rooster crowed, and all together they made such a dreadful noise that they frightened the robbers clean away.

Jack and the animals went inside the house. Jack was afraid, though, that the robbers would come back in the middle of the night, so he put the cat in the rocking chair, and he put the dog under the table, and he put the goat upstairs, and he put the bull down in the cellar. Jack told the rooster to fly up on the roof, and then he got into bed.

By and by, the robbers saw that the house was dark, so they sent one man back to fetch the money. Well, before long the man came running back, breathless with fright, and told this story:

"I went back to the house," he said, "and I went in, and I tried to sit down in the rocking chair, and there was a woman knitting, and she stuck her knitting needles into me!"

That was the cat, you know.

"I went to the table to find our money, and there was a carpenter under the table, and he started to saw on my leg!"

That was the dog, you know.

"I ran upstairs to the attic, and there was a giant up there, and he hit me with his two hard fists!"

That was the mule, you know.

"I ran downstairs to the cellar, but there was a man down there chopping wood, and he cut me with his ax!"

That was the bull, you know.

"I ran outside, and there was a devil up on the roof shouting, "Toss him up to meeee! Toss him up to meeee!"

That was the rooster, you know.

Those robbers went far away, and don't you know, they left all their money behind in the house. Jack and his companions reckoned they had found their fortune, and they lived in that house for the rest of their days.

MEDIO POLLITO

Argentina

There was an old woman who was so poor that all she had in the world was one scrawny hen. One day the hen laid a little egg, and to the woman's surprise, the chick that hatched from the egg had only one wing and one leg.

"My hen laid just one egg, and my little chick is only half a chick," grumbled the old woman. "Poor people always have bad luck."

The woman called the chick Medio Pollito—Half Chick—and she fed him and took care of him. Although he was only half a chick, he had a huge appetite, and all day long he cried, "*Peep, peep, peep!* Give me something good to eat!"

The old woman fed Medio Pollito until there was no food left in the house. "Shoo! Go and find your own supper," she told him.

Medio Pollito hopped all around the neighborhood, looking for something to eat. What did he find? A golden orange! He took it to the old woman, crying, "*Peep, peep, peep!* Look at this golden orange. I will take it to the king and trade it for wheat, and then we will have plenty to eat."

Medio Pollito put the golden orange under his one wing and hopped along the road on his one leg.

Medio Pollito met a fox.

"Where are you going, Medio Pollito?" the fox asked.

"*Peep, peep, peep!* I'm going to see the king and trade this golden orange for a bushel of wheat."

"May I go with you?" asked the fox.

"Yes," said Medio Pollito. "Jump in my mouth, and tap yourself with my magic stick."

Medio Pollito opened his beak, and in jumped the fox. *Tap, tap, tap,* went the magic stick. The fox became very small. He rode along happily in Medio Pollito's stomach, and the little chick hopped along the road to the king's palace.

Medio Pollito met a tiger.

"Where are you going, Medio Pollito?" the tiger asked.

"*Peep, peep, peep,*" said the chick. "I am going to see the king and trade this golden orange for a bushel of wheat."

"May I go with you?" asked the tiger.

"Yes," said Medio Pollito. "Jump in my mouth, and tap yourself with my magic stick."

Medio Pollito opened his beak, and in jumped the tiger. *Tap, tap, tap,* went the magic stick. The tiger became very, very small. He and the fox rode along very happily in Medio Pollito's stomach, and the little chick hopped along the road to the king's palace.

Medio Pollito came to a river.

"Where are you going, Medio Pollito?" asked the river.

"*Peep, peep, peep,*" said the chick. "I am going to see the king and trade this golden orange for a bushel of wheat."

"May I go with you?" asked the river.

"Yes," said Medio Pollito. "Jump in my mouth, and tap yourself with my magic stick."

Medio Pollito bent down and opened his beak, and in flowed the river. *Tap, tap, tap,* went the magic stick, and the river became very, very small. The river and the tiger and the fox rode along happily in Medio Pollito's stomach, and the little chick hopped along the road to the king's palace.

The king was delighted to see Medio Pollito's golden orange. "You may have this golden orange," the chick told him, "if you give me a bushel of wheat."

The king took the golden orange, and then he called his guards. "Throw this little chick in the hen house," said the king. "Imagine—half a chick telling me what to do!"

The king's guards threw Medio Pollito into the hen house. All the hens looked at Medio Pollito and clucked, "He is not one of us. Peck him! Peck him! Peck him!"

"Brother Fox," peeped Medio Pollito. "It's time to grow large again."

Tap, tap, tap, went the magic stick. The fox sprang out of Medio Pollito's beak and chased the chickens all around the hen house while Medio Pollito escaped. The little chick marched up to the door of the palace once again, crying, "*Peep, peep, peep.* Give me my wheat!"

The king called his guards again. "Throw this miserable half a chick into the stable with the mules," he commanded.

The king's guards grabbed Medio Pollito and tossed him into the stable, where the mules began to kick the little chick around like a soccer ball.

"Brother Tiger!" peeped Medio Pollito. "It's time to grow large again."

Tap, tap, tap, went the magic stick. The tiger sprang out of Medio Pollito's beak, and the mules were so frightened they broke down the stable door and ran away.

Medio Pollito hopped to the palace, crying, "*Peep, peep, peep.* Give me my wheat!"

"Guards!" cried the king. "Tell the royal cook to bake this half a chick for my supper."

The guards carried Medio Pollito to the royal cook, and the royal cook put him in a pan, and buttered him, and sprinkled him with spices, and put him into the oven.

The inside of the oven was so hot! "Sister River," peeped Medio Pollito. "It's time to grow large again."

Tap, tap, tap, went the magic stick. The river flowed out of Medio Pollito's beak, and quenched the fire in the oven, and burst open the oven door, and flooded the king's palace. Medio Pollito floated in his little pan to the king's chamber, where the king had climbed up the curtains and was hanging from the chandelier.

"Take all the wheat you want!" said the king to Medio Pollito. "Take a cart, and take a horse, and take the wheat, and go away, and never come back."

That is exactly what Medio Pollito did. He loaded a cart with wheat and drove the cart back to the old woman's house, and neither of them was ever hungry again. They sold some of the wheat, and planted some of the wheat, and lived very well for the rest of their days.

MASTER THUMB

Burma/Myanmar

There was once a woman who was expecting a child, and one day she set a basket of rice to dry in the sun. No sooner had she set the basket down than it began to rain. So the woman carried the basket inside her house. But as soon as she did, the sun came out again. And so it went—whenever she put her rice basket outside, the rain began to fall, and whenever she took her rice basket inside, the sun began to shine. In and out, in and out she went, until at last she said some angry words to the sun.

"How dare you speak to me like that!" the sun said to her. "I will put a curse on you. The child you are carrying will never grow larger than your thumb."

So it came to pass that the woman had a baby boy no bigger than her thumb, and he never grew at all. The other children called him Master Thumb and made fun of him, and so he was always very sad.

When he was sixteen years old, the boy demanded to know

why he was so small, and his mother told him about the sun's curse.

"Mother, bake me a cake," said Master Thumb. "Tomorrow I am going to find the sun and ask him to remove the curse."

Early the next morning, Master Thumb left home carrying the cake, which was many times bigger than himself.

It was midsummer. The fields were brown, and the heat of the sun was fierce. By and by, Master Thumb met Wooden Boat, who was stuck in the dry riverbed.

"Where are you going, Master Thumb?" asked Wooden Boat.

"I am going to ask the sun to remove his curse, so that I can grow tall."

"I would like to ask the sun to send rain, so that I can float in the river again," said Wooden Boat.

"Why don't you come with me?" said Master Thumb. "Eat some of my cake and jump into my stomach."

Wooden Boat took a bite of Master Thumb's cake, and became quite small, and jumped into Master Thumb's stomach, and Master Thumb kept marching along the road. After a while, he met Bamboo Thorn.

"Where are you going, Master Thumb?" asked Bamboo Thorn.

"I am going to ask the sun to remove his curse, so that I can grow tall."

"May I go with you?" asked Bamboo Thorn. "I would like to ask the sun to send rain so that the bamboo can grow."

"Yes, come with me," said Master Thumb. "Eat some of my cake and jump into my stomach."

Bamboo Thorn took a bite of Master Thumb's cake, and became quite small, and jumped into Master Thumb's stomach, and Master Thumb kept marching along the road. After a while, he met Cow Pat.

"Where are you going, Master Thumb?" asked Cow Pat.

"I am going to ask the sun to remove his curse, so that I can grow tall."

"I would like to ask the sun to cool down," said Cow Pat. "All the cows are thirsty and sad."

"Come with me," said Master Thumb. "Eat some of my cake and jump into my stomach."

Cow Pat took a bite of Master Thumb's cake, and became quite small, and slid into Master Thumb's stomach, and Master Thumb kept walking along the road. After a bit, he met Rotten Egg.

"Where are you going, Master Thumb?" asked Rotten Egg.

"I am going to ask the sun to remove his curse, so that I can grow tall."

"The sun has dried up the water, and the roosters and hens and chicks have nothing to drink," said Rotten Egg. "I would like to ask the sun to let the rain fall."

"Why don't you come with me?" said Master Thumb. "Eat some of my cake and jump into my stomach."

Rotten Egg took a bite of Master Thumb's cake, and became

quite small, and rolled into Master Thumb's stomach, and Master Thumb kept walking along the road.

After a long, long journey, Master Thumb came to the edge of the world, where the sun's house stood. And because the sun was still traveling across the sky, his house was empty. Master Thumb went inside.

"Come out, my friends," said Master Thumb. "Wooden Boat, get behind the house. Bamboo Thorn, you lie down in the sun's bed. Cow Pat, sit in the middle of the floor. Rotten Egg, roll into the ashes of the fire."

Master Thumb hid in a dark corner and waited.

Soon afterward, the sun came home. He walked wearily through the door and sank down onto the bed. *Bing!* Bamboo Thorn poked the sun's cheek.

"Ooh! Ah!" shouted the sun. "Something has bitten my cheek. I must rub ashes on it."

The sun ran to the fireplace. He put his hands in the ashes, but when he did, Rotten Egg burst, shooting sharp pieces of eggshell into his eyes and making a horrible stink. The sun screamed, took a step backward, and stepped on Cow Pat. Whoops! He slipped and fell flat on the floor.

"Is there some kind of demon in my house?" howled the sun. "Go away, whoever you are."

Then Master Thumb stepped forward and said, "I will go away if you take back the curse you put on a baby boy sixteen years ago, that he would never grow bigger than his mother's thumb."

"Yes, yes!" moaned the sun. "I take it away. It's gone."

"And you must send rain to his country, so that the rivers flow, and the plants grow, and the animals have food and water."

"You want rain, do you?" roared the sun. "I will send you rain!"

Rain began to fall so hard that a torrent rolled toward the sun's house. Quickly, Master Thumb jumped into Wooden Boat, and he rode the raging water all the way to his village. Everyone welcomed Master Thumb, who by then had grown quite tall and who brought with him the wonderful rain.

CAN YOU GUESS MY NAME?

Tales like "Rumpelstiltskin"

Belief in the magical power of names is ancient and widespread. According to folk belief, to know a person's name—especially a person's *secret* name—confers control over him or her. In traditional societies, adults warned children never to tell their names to a stranger, recounting the sad fates of those who did. Tales about guessing names also satisfy children's keen interest in keeping, telling, and guessing secrets. The secret names in the following tales are made-up nonsense words, and so they are virtually impossible to guess. But everyone knows that secrets are difficult, if not impossible, to keep.

TITELITURE

Sweden

There was once a poor woman who had an only daughter, and the girl was so lazy that she refused to turn her hand to any work whatsoever. This caused her mother no end of grief. The woman tried time and again to teach her daughter how to spin, but it was of no use. Finally, the mother made the girl sit on the thatched roof of their cottage with her spinning wheel. "Now the whole world can see what a lazy, good-for-nothing daughter you are," said the woman.

That very afternoon, the king's son came riding by the house on his way home from the hunt. He was surprised to see such a beautiful young woman sitting on a cottage roof. He asked the girl's mother why she was there.

The woman was tongue-tied. How could she tell him the truth? "O-o-oh," she stammered. "My daughter is on the roof because . . . because she is such a clever girl, she can spin the long straw on the roof into pure gold."

"Aha!" cried the prince. "If what you say is true, and this maiden *can* spin gold from straw, she must come to the palace and be my bride." So the girl came down from the roof and mounted the prince's horse behind him, and off they rode.

When they reached the palace, the queen led the girl to a small tower room, and gave her a spinning wheel and a great tall pile of straw, and said, "If you can spin this into gold by the time the sun rises, you shall be my son's bride. But if you have deceived us, you will pay with your life."

The poor girl was terribly afraid, for of course she had never learned to spin thread, let alone gold. There she sat, her head in her hands, crying bitter tears, when the door to the room slowly opened and in walked in an odd-looking little man. He greeted her in a friendly way and asked why she was crying.

"I have good reason to cry," answered the girl. "The queen has ordered me to spin this straw into gold before dawn, or I shall pay with my life. No one can spin straw into gold."

"No one?" asked the little man. He held out a glove that sparkled and shimmered in the candlelight. "As long as you wear this, *you* will be able to spin it all into gold. But there is a price for using my glove. Tomorrow night I shall return and ask you to guess my name. If you cannot guess it, you must marry me and be my wife."

In her despair, the girl made the bargain. As soon as the little man disappeared, she put on the glove, and sat and spun as if she had been spinning her whole life. By sunrise she had spun all the straw into the finest gold.

Great was the joy of everyone in the palace that the prince had found a bride who was so beautiful and so skillful. The maiden did not rejoice, though, but sat by the window and strained to think what the little man's name might be.

When the prince returned from the hunt, he sat down, and to amuse her he began to tell her of his adventures that day. "I saw the strangest thing in the forest," he said. "I came to a clearing, and there was little old man dancing round and round a juniper bush, singing the most peculiar song."

"What did he sing?" asked the maiden.

The prince replied,

> "My bride must sew her wedding dress,
> Because she used my magic glove,
> And she will never, ever guess
> Titeliture's the name of her love."

The girl smiled and clapped her hands, and asked the prince to sing the little man's song over and over so that she wouldn't forget. And when the prince left her alone, and night fell, the door to her chamber opened. There stood the little old man, grinning from ear to ear. Before he could say a word, the girl held out the glove, saying, "Here is your glove . . . *Titeliture!*"

When the little man heard her speak his name, he shrieked and he spun around and around, and then, with a bang and a great puff of smoke, he shot up through the air and disappeared, taking part of the tower roof with him.

The girl and the prince were married, and never again did she have to spin, because, of course, spinning is not proper work for a princess.

HOW IJAPA THE TORTOISE TRICKED THE HIPPOPOTAMUS

Nigeria: Yoruba

The story floats in the air. It hovers. Where will it land? It falls upon Ijapa, the tortoise. He is small, yet he tricked the powerful hippopotamus.

Today the hippopotamus lives in the water, where he is ruler of no one. But long ago he lived on dry land and was a mighty chief, second only to the elephant. A curious thing about the hippopotamus was that, apart his family, no one knew his name. He had seven wives, each as big and plump as he, and his wives were the only ones, besides the hippopotamus himself, who knew what he was called.

The hippopotamus and his wives enjoyed nothing more than eating. They would invite all the other animals to dine with them, and then, just as the feasting was about to begin, the hippopotamus would say, "You have come to feed at my table—yes, you have, yes, you have—but who among you knows my name? No one should eat my food or drink my wine if he does not know my name."

Not one of the animals knew the name of the hippopotamus. What could they do? A few of them would guess, but their guesses were always wrong. Time and again, they went away hungry, until at last Ijapa the tortoise could stand it no longer.

"You say that if we guess your name, you will let us eat your food," said Ijapa. "That is not enough. I think you should do something very big, very important, if we guess your name."

"No one will *ever* guess my name!" bellowed the hippopotamus. "But if you do, I promise I will leave the land and go live in the water, and so will all of my family."

It was the custom of the hippopotamus and his seven wives to bathe in the river each morning. Ijapa the tortoise hid in the underbrush and watched them come and go, day after day. He noticed that one of the hippo's wives walked more slowly than the rest and was always the last to leave the river.

One morning, Ijapa waited for all of the hippos to walk down to the river. Then, while they were washing and drinking, Ijapa dug a hole in the middle of the path. He lowered himself into the hole so that his shell looked like a smooth, worn rock. He waited as the hippo and the first six wives clomped back up the path. Then, before the seventh wife came, he rolled onto his side. His shell stuck up out of the hole. Sure enough, hippo wife number seven tripped on Ijapa's shell. She crashed to the ground and rolled onto her back.

"Help!" she shouted. "I can't get up! Isantim, my husband! Come quickly! Help! Isantim!"

While the hippopotamus helped wife number seven onto her feet, Ijapa the tortoise walked home, repeating "Isantim, Isantim, Isantim." From morning till night he said the word to himself softly, so that no one else could hear, "Isantim, Isantim, Isantim."

At his next feast, the hippopotamus proclaimed as usual, "You have come to feed at my table—yes, you have, yes, you have—but who among you knows my name? No one should eat my food or drink my wine if he does not know my name."

Ijapa cleared his throat, *hem, hem*. Then he said, "Be quiet, Isantim, and let me eat."

The hippopotamus's mouth dropped open. He was speechless. A cheer went up from all the animals, "Hooray for Ijapa!" They sat down and ate Isantim's food and drank Isantim's palm wine.

When the feast was over, Isantim and his wives carried all their belongings to the river. That is where they live today, because Isantim allowed himself to be tricked by Ijapa the tortoise.

ONIROKU

Japan

High in the mountains of Japan there flowed a raging river that surged and whirled around rocks and boulders. Since the beginning of time, there had been no way to cross that river, whether on foot, or on horseback, or in a boat. The people who lived near the river had tried again and again to build a bridge, but each time, the river's powerful currents brought their handiwork crashing down.

In a faraway city there lived a man who was rumored to be the finest builder in all of Japan. His fame spread throughout the country until at last news of his great skill reached the people who lived in the village beside the river. They sent a messenger, offering whatever price he asked to build a bridge for them.

The master builder came at once, eager to test his skill. He stood on the riverbank looking out at the whirlpools and waterfalls that he would have to conquer, and he thought, "There is no bridge that will withstand the power of this river. Yet if I do not build one here, my reputation will be ruined."

As the builder pondered his situation, an oni—a hideous horned ogre—arose from the river—*tsaan!* The oni's long, tangled hair swirled about him, and his enormous eyes flashed like lightning.

"You can never build a bridge here," thundered the oni, "unless you have my help. I bring them all down, yes. I bring them *all* crashing down."

The builder began to tremble and shake. Then the oni spoke again: "If you should agree to pay my price, I will not only allow a bridge to be built here, I will build it myself, tonight, while you sleep."

How much money would the oni want, the master builder wondered. The people of the village had offered him any price he asked. "Very well," he told the oni, "I will pay your price." Then he went to a local inn for the night, but the uneasy memory of making a bargain with an oni kept him awake for a long time.

The next morning, the builder hurried to the spot where he had met the oni. There, to his great astonishment, a magnificent wooden bridge, high and strong, arched above the wild currents of the river. At the foot of the bridge stood the oni, smiling and showing his gruesome yellow tusks.

"And now for my payment," he said. "You must give me your eyes!"

"My eyes?" the master builder cried out in anguish. "No! No!" How had he fallen into the oni's trap so easily? He dropped to his knees and pleaded with the monster, tears streaming down his cheeks.

"Oh, very well," said the oni at last. "Since you carry on in this disgusting manner, I will give you one chance to escape your fate. If by sunset you have learned my name, you may keep your eyes. If not, they are mine!"

The oni strode onto the bridge, jumped over the side—*tsaan!*—and sank beneath the swirling rapids.

The builder turned and ran into the forest. He had no idea how he could ever discover the name of the oni. Deeper and deeper he plunged into the silent woods.

Then he heard the sound of drumming and the footsteps of dancers—*tangura, tangura, tangura, tangura.* He walked toward the noise and found a clearing among the trees where six or seven little oni children were dancing and clapping their paws, and singing,

"When Oniroku brings the eyes,
How happy we will be!
When Oniroku brings the eyes,
How happy we will be!"

The builder's heart pounded with joy and excitement. He turned and ran back to the river.

"Oniroku! Oniroku!" he shouted. "Where are you, Oniroku?"

The water churned and bubbled—*tsaan!* The oni's hideous face appeared in the water.

"How did you learn my name?" the oni raged. "Who told you my name?" His face turned crimson and great gusts of steam shot from his nose and mouth. At last, he regained his composure. "Keep your silly eyes," he rumbled. "But never tell my name to anyone else, and do not ever dare come back here again."

You may be sure that the master builder never did.

I MARRIED A FROG

Tales like "The Frog Prince"

"The Frog Prince," from the German collection of the Brothers Grimm, is one of the best-known European folktales. Parts of the story seem to be missing, though. How did the prince become a frog in the first place? Does he really deserve to marry a princess? The tellers of similar tales from other cultures answer these questions. In the Swazi folktale "Princess Tombi-ende and the Frog," it was a cruel monster who transformed a noble young man into a frog. In the Hmong tale "How a Warty Toad Became an Emperor" and in "Little Singing Frog" from Serbia, a boy and a girl are born in animal form because of mistakes their parents made. In each of these tales, as in most folktales of animal brides and grooms, the enchanted creatures win their partners not by demanding a kiss but by showing wisdom, skill, and courage. Oddly enough, their human spouses do not find them repulsive in their animal forms. Frogginess and toadliness, it seems, are in the eye of the beholder.

PRINCESS TOMBI-ENDE AND THE FROG

Swaziland

Tombi-ende was the most beautiful girl in her father's kingdom. She had milk-white teeth and sparkling eyes and a graceful walk, so that you could not help noticing her among her many sisters. She was taller than the others, and she carried her head like a true princess. Her mother and father looked upon her with joy and pride, knowing that one day she would become a mighty queen.

Time passed, and Tombi-ende's sisters grew more and more jealous of her. As long as *she* was around, they said to each other, no one would ever notice *them*. They made a plan to get rid of her, and one morning they asked her to go with them to dig red ochre at the clay pit. The sisters walked along together, singing and laughing. When they reached the pit, they jumped in and began to dig.

"Tombi-ende, the best clay is down there, in the deepest part of the pit," said her sisters. "Why don't you dig there?"

When she did, they threw clay at her until she was completely buried. Then the sisters ran home, crying and shouting, "Tombi-ende fell in the clay pit and we cannot find her!"

The king sent Tombi-ende's brothers to search for her. At the clay pit, they heard a voice calling,

"I am Tombi-ende,
I am not dead,
I am like one of you."

But although they dug everywhere in the red clay, they could not find their sister, and after many long days of searching, they returned home. Everyone gave up hope for Tombi-ende.

Time passed. Tombi-ende's body rose up through the clay and reached the surface. She was alive, but so weak from hunger and thirst that she could not move. Two bright eyes gazed down at her from the edge of the pit, and a deep voice said, "Beautiful princess, what are you doing here?"

Tombi-ende looked up and saw a giant frog. "My sisters brought me here," she told him. "They threw clay on me and left me for dead."

"Let me help you," said the frog. "Don't be afraid." He jumped down into the pit, opened his mouth, and swallowed her—not a moment too soon! An inzimu, a cannibal monster, came running along the path to the clay pit. He was looking for

Tombi-ende, for he had heard that the girl was still alive, and he wanted to eat her. But the inzimu paid no attention to the frog as he hopped past.

The frog carried Tombi-ende as far as her grandmother's village, croaking, "I carry Tombi-ende, the beautiful princess."

"Who is speaking?" asked the grandmother. "Who knows what has become of my darling Tombi-ende?"

"Woo-oo-oh!" croaked the frog. *"Woo-oo-oh!"* And there stood Tombi-ende, tall and beautiful. Everyone was so pleased, and they couldn't hear her tale too often or praise the frog too much for what he had done.

"How can we ever repay you?" the grandmother asked the frog.

"Hold a feast for us," said the frog, "and let me sit and eat beside the princess." So it was done, but the next morning, when Tombi-ende looked for the frog, she found that he had disappeared.

Tombi-ende's grandmother sent for the girl's brothers to come and escort her home. Now, when Tombi-ende and her brothers were walking along, it became very hot. They were thirsty, but they could find no water, for every stream and spring was dry. They grew so weak that they collapsed to the ground.

A tall man appeared before them.

"Do you know where we can find water?" Tombi-ende's brothers asked the man.

"I have plenty of water," said the tall man. "I will give it to you, but what will you give me in return?"

"We will give you anything in our father's kingdom," said the brothers.

"I want this beautiful princess," said the man, with a wicked smile. "You might as well give her to me, because if you don't, all of you will die of thirst."

The brothers had no choice but to agree. The man led them to a fig tree beside a dry riverbed. He struck ground near the tree with a stick, and water flowed forth, as cool and clear as moonlight. Tombi-ende and her brothers bent down and drank handfuls of the water. When they looked up again, they saw that the tall stranger was not a man at all, but a monstrous and misshapen inzimu, with one huge leg, a tail, and long, sharp teeth.

Suddenly, a noise came from the water: *"Woo-oo-oh!"*

"It is my hero," said Tombi-ende. "Please help us, dear frog!"

The frog leapt forward and opened his mouth wide. *"Woo-oo-oh!"* He swallowed the inzimu and dived into the pool. He stayed under the water until the inzimu had drowned. Then he hopped out again.

"How can I ever thank you?" cried the princess. "This time you must not disappear. Please come home with us."

Tombi-ende's father and mother were so happy to see her alive and well. "But why is this disgusting frog standing next to you?" her father asked. "Guards, kill him."

"No!" shouted Tombi-ende. "This frog saved my life twice, and I love him."

Instantly, a tall, handsome young man stood before her. He

carried a shield and a spear, and wore a headdress of ostrich feathers.

"I am not a frog," he told the king. "My father was a great king, like yourself, but the inzimu of the fig tree destroyed him and enchanted me. I had to remain a frog until I won the love of a fair maiden. I can give you many cattle in exchange for your daughter's hand in marriage."

The king and queen were so happy that they forgave Tombiende's wicked sisters, and the princess and her prince were married and lived happily together for a long time.

HOW A WARTY TOAD BECAME AN EMPEROR

China: Hmong

It happened once long ago that a woman gave birth not to a baby but to a warty toad. She wanted to toss the child into the swamp with the other toads, but her husband said no, it was their duty to raise him as their own son, and so they did. One day, when the toad was nearly grown, there was to be a great festival in his grandfather's village. The toad asked his parents if he could accompany them.

"Don't be silly," said his mother. "People would laugh at you. Stay at home and mind the house."

"I am not afraid of people laughing at me," said the toad. "I want to go with you."

The toad hopped along behind his mother and father, and at the festival he met a beautiful girl. They talked together for a long time, and she let him walk her home. Later the toad told his parents, "That is the girl I want to marry. Please ask her father for me."

"You are hideous," said his mother. "No one would marry a toad. If we ask the girl's father, he will laugh at us."

"I am not afraid of people laughing," said the toad. "Doesn't her father owe our family many favors? I insist that you ask him."

The toad's parents went to the girl's house and asked for her hand in marriage. The girl's father did not dare refuse outright. Instead, he told them, "I am not sure that your son will be able to work on the farm, since he is only a toad. Before I agree to the marriage, your son must perform three tasks for me."

The toad went to the girl's house, and on the first day her father led him to a tall cliff and pointed to a tree growing at the very edge. "Chop this tree down, cut it into firewood, and bring it to my house," he commanded. Then, when the toad turned and began to chop the tree, the man pushed him over the edge of the cliff and ran home. Imagine his surprise when, a few hours later, the toad appeared at the door carrying a tall stack of firewood.

"We will need fresh water for the wedding," said the toad's future father-in-law the next morning. "There is a spring not far from here, and beside the spring you will find a water jar. Bring the jar to me." Now, the jar was a huge stone jar, and it was much too heavy to lift. It was there only to collect water, and no one ever carried it. The man secretly hoped that the jar would crush the toad, and he would be rid of this unwelcome suitor. Imagine his surprise when the toad appeared a few moments later, balancing the stone jar on his head as if it were made of straw.

"We will be serving rice at your wedding," said the toad's future father-in-law the next day. "You must harvest all of my rice before sunset."

The man's fields were so vast that no one person could hope to harvest them in a week, much less in a day, but the toad set out cheerfully, carrying several scythes with him. Later, when his sweetheart brought his lunch to him, she was amazed to see the toad resting in the shade of a tree while the scythes were cutting the rice all by themselves at a furious pace. Soon after she arrived, all the rice was harvested, and the toad carried it to her father's house.

Afterward, the toad and his sweetheart were married, and whenever they were alone together, the toad would turn a somersault, step out of his toad's skin, and became a handsome young man. But whenever they were going to be around other people, he would somersault back into the skin and become a toad again.

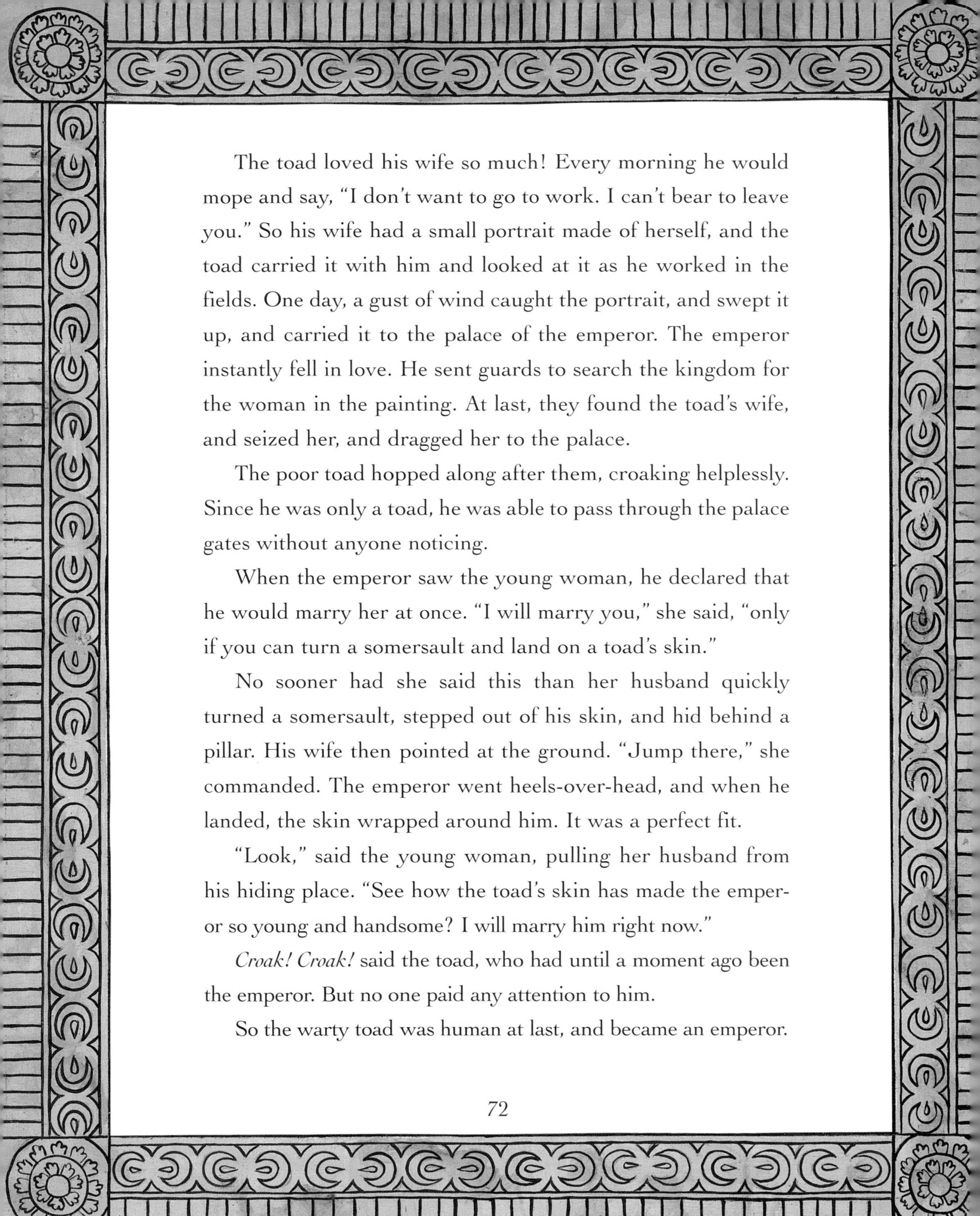

The toad loved his wife so much! Every morning he would mope and say, "I don't want to go to work. I can't bear to leave you." So his wife had a small portrait made of herself, and the toad carried it with him and looked at it as he worked in the fields. One day, a gust of wind caught the portrait, and swept it up, and carried it to the palace of the emperor. The emperor instantly fell in love. He sent guards to search the kingdom for the woman in the painting. At last, they found the toad's wife, and seized her, and dragged her to the palace.

The poor toad hopped along after them, croaking helplessly. Since he was only a toad, he was able to pass through the palace gates without anyone noticing.

When the emperor saw the young woman, he declared that he would marry her at once. "I will marry you," she said, "only if you can turn a somersault and land on a toad's skin."

No sooner had she said this than her husband quickly turned a somersault, stepped out of his skin, and hid behind a pillar. His wife then pointed at the ground. "Jump there," she commanded. The emperor went heels-over-head, and when he landed, the skin wrapped around him. It was a perfect fit.

"Look," said the young woman, pulling her husband from his hiding place. "See how the toad's skin has made the emperor so young and handsome? I will marry him right now."

Croak! Croak! said the toad, who had until a moment ago been the emperor. But no one paid any attention to him.

So the warty toad was human at last, and became an emperor.

LITTLE SINGING FROG

Serbia

There once lived a poor couple who had no children. Every day the woman would sigh and say, "How I wish we had a child!" Then the man too would sigh and say, "It would be nice to have a little daughter, wouldn't it?"

"I would like any kind of a child!" said the woman. "Even if it were a frog."

Soon their wish came true, and they had a little daughter. Not a little girl daughter, though—a little *frog* daughter. Still, they loved their frog child dearly, and they doted on her, and played with her, and laughed and clapped their hands as they watched her hopping about the house.

But the neighbors whispered, "Why, that child of theirs is nothing but a frog." Then the man and woman grew ashamed. They decided to keep their frog child hidden in a closet.

The man worked in a vineyard, and every day at noontime

the woman carried his dinner to him in a basket. As the years went by, the basket seemed to grow heavier and heavier, and it took the woman longer and longer to make the trip to the vineyard.

"Let me help you, Mother," said the little frog. "Let me carry Father's dinner to him while you sit at home and rest."

From that time on, the frog girl carried her father's dinner basket to the vineyard. While the man ate, his daughter would hop up into the branches of a tree and sing to him. She sang so sweetly, her father called her his Little Singing Frog.

One day, the tsar's youngest son rode by and heard her song. He stopped his horse and looked this way and that, but for the life of him he couldn't tell where the music was coming from.

"Who is singing?" he asked the old man.

The old man, who was ashamed of his frog daughter, pretended not to hear him. When the young prince repeated his question, the old man answered gruffly, "No one is singing!"

The next day at the same hour, the prince rode by again, and heard the same sweet voice. He stopped and listened. "Surely someone is singing," he said to the old man. "It's a lovely girl, I know it is! Why, if I could find her, I'd be willing to marry her at once and take her home to my father the tsar."

"Don't be rash," the old man warned him.

"I mean what I say!" the prince declared. "I would marry her in a minute!"

"Are you sure?"

"Yes, I'm sure!"

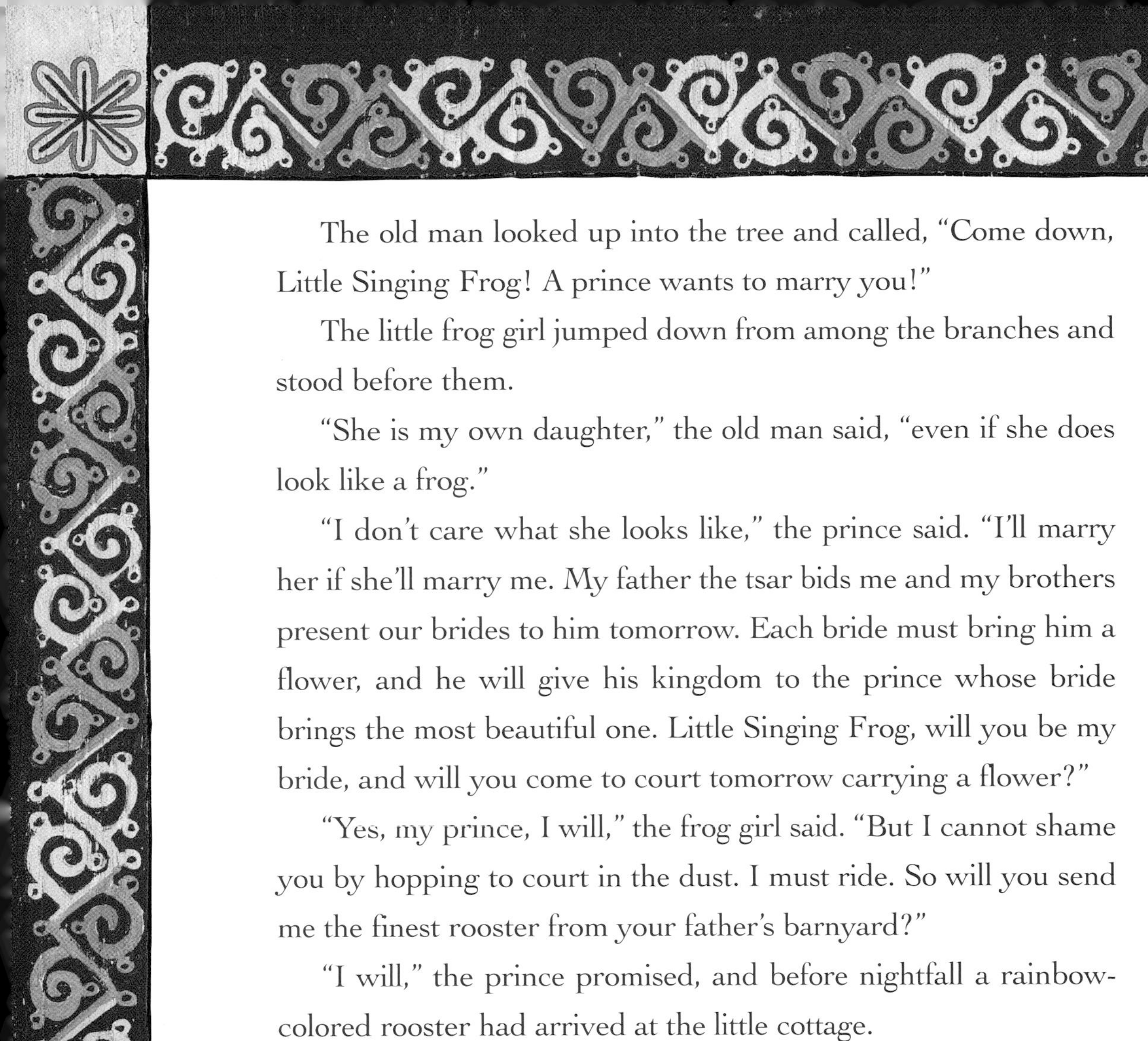

The old man looked up into the tree and called, "Come down, Little Singing Frog! A prince wants to marry you!"

The little frog girl jumped down from among the branches and stood before them.

"She is my own daughter," the old man said, "even if she does look like a frog."

"I don't care what she looks like," the prince said. "I'll marry her if she'll marry me. My father the tsar bids me and my brothers present our brides to him tomorrow. Each bride must bring him a flower, and he will give his kingdom to the prince whose bride brings the most beautiful one. Little Singing Frog, will you be my bride, and will you come to court tomorrow carrying a flower?"

"Yes, my prince, I will," the frog girl said. "But I cannot shame you by hopping to court in the dust. I must ride. So will you send me the finest rooster from your father's barnyard?"

"I will," the prince promised, and before nightfall a rainbow-colored rooster had arrived at the little cottage.

The next morning, at dawn, Little Singing Frog went outside and danced in the sun's first rays, and the sun sent down a golden dress, which the frog girl folded until it was very small. Instead of a flower, she took a spear of wheat in her hand, and when the time was right, she sat astride the rooster and rode to the palace.

The guards at the palace gate at first refused to admit her. "This is no place for frogs!" they said, and laughed. "You must be looking for a pond!"

But when she told them she was the bride of the youngest prince, the guards let her ride through the gate. "How strange," they murmured to one another. "The youngest prince's bride looks exactly like a frog! And wasn't that a rooster she was riding?" Stepping inside the gates to look at her again, they beheld a marvelous sight. The frog girl shook out the folds of the golden gown and dropped the gown over her head. Instantly, the frog and the rooster disappeared, and the guards beheld a lovely maiden mounted on a rainbow-colored horse.

Little Singing Frog entered the palace with two other girls, the promised brides of the older princes. They were just ordinary girls, both of them. To see them you wouldn't have paid any attention to them one way or the other, but standing beside the lovely bride of the youngest prince, they seemed dull and drab indeed. All three were led to the chamber of the tsar.

The first girl stepped forward, holding a rose in her hand. The tsar looked at the rose, and looked at her, and shook his head. The second girl held out a carnation. The tsar looked at her for a moment and murmured, "Dear me, no." Then he looked at the youngest prince's bride. His eyes twinkled as she gave him the spear of wheat. He took it and held it aloft. Then he reached out his other hand to her and had her stand beside him as he said to his sons and all the court, "The bride of the youngest prince is my choice. See how beautiful she is! And she knows that true beauty nourishes, for as her flower she has chosen a spear of wheat! The youngest prince shall be the tsar after me, and she shall be tsarina."

So Little Singing Frog, whose parents were so ashamed of her, married the youngest prince, and when the time came, she wore a tsarina's crown.

THE SCARY HOUSE IN THE BIG WOODS

Tales like "Hansel and Gretel"

Storytellers the world over spin tales of children who encounter terrifying cannibal monsters. The monsters in these tales are very much alike from culture to culture: large of body but small of brain. Slow thinkers, most can easily be duped into destroying themselves. How the children fall into the monsters' clutches differs from tale to tale. Few are abandoned in the woods by their parents; they are far more likely either to be kidnapped by the monster or to wander into the woods of their own accord. The children overcome the monster and escape by running fast and climbing high, by earning the help of animals and friendly adults, and by taking advantage of their enemy's poor eyesight and gullibility.

JEAN AND JEANNETTE

France

Once upon a time, in a small cottage near the edge of a forest, there lived a man and a woman who were very poor, and they had two children, named Jean and Jeannette. Jean was twelve and Jeannette was a few years younger, and the two of them loved each other dearly.

One evening, after the children were in bed, the mother said to the father, "We have nothing left to eat in the house but a handful of flour. I'll make a little round bun with it. Tomorrow you will give it to the children, and take them to the forest, and leave them there. Someone is sure to find them and take care of them."

The next day, their father put the bun in his pocket and told the children to come with him, for he was going to gather firewood. He led them to a clearing in the forest, and climbed up a little hill, and said, "Do you see this little bun? I'm going to let it roll down the hill, and whoever catches it may eat it."

He did just that, and the bun rolled deep into the woods. The children ran after it, laughing and shouting.

Jean got there first and picked up the bun. He split it down the middle with his little knife and gave half to Jeannette, and after they had eaten it, they looked for birds' nests and made whistles and picked flowers and had a lovely time. Then they began to miss their father. "Papa, where are you?" they called, but there was no answer.

"Don't worry, little sister," said Jean. "I'll climb a tree and look for our house."

Jean scrambled up a tall pine tree.

"Can you see it?" asked Jeannette.

"No," said Jean, "but I see a red house and a white house."

"Throw your hat," said Jeannette, "and we will go where it goes."

Jean tossed his hat, and the wind carried it toward the red house.

Now, the red house was an ogre's house, and when Jean and Jeannette knocked at the door, a huge, horrible woman appeared. She wore a bonnet on her head, and the children thought they could see a little horn poking out at either side.

"Dear Madame," said Jean, trembling a bit, "may we sleep here tonight?"

"Why, yes, of course," said the ogress excitedly. "My husband will be so happy to meet you. Come in. Sit down by the fire and have a crust of bread and some cheese."

After they had eaten as much as they could, Jean and Jeannette lay down on a bed near the fire and fell asleep. In the middle of the night, the ogre came stomping through the door. "Hey, hey! What do I smell?" he growled. He went to the bed, pulled back the covers, and picked up Jean and Jeannette, one by the arm and one by the leg.

"Look what I've found!" cried the ogre, smiling and showing his sharp yellow teeth. "A girl to be our servant, and a boy who'll make a fine supper—after I put him in the pigsty and fatten him up a bit. He is much too skinny to eat now."

Every morning, Jeannette took food to her brother in the pigsty, and every evening the ogre went to see the boy. He would ask Jean to stick out his finger, so that he could tell how fat he was getting. Jean caught a mouse and cut off its tail, and he stuck it through the little door of the pigsty. The ogre, whose eyesight was not very good, squeezed the mouse tail. "Too thin!" he roared.

In this way, for many weeks, Jean fooled the ogre, but at last one evening the ogre was so hungry that he said to the ogress, "Fat, thin—I don't care. Cook that boy tonight! I'm going to visit my ogre friends, and when I return, I want him baked in a pie."

The ogress went to the pigsty and pulled Jean into the house by his ear. "Up on the chopping block now, my pet," she told him. "Time to cut off your head."

"But I don't know how to get up on the chopping block," said Jean. "Could you show me how?"

"Imbecile!" the ogress screamed. "You just climb up like this," and she did, "and put your head down like this," and she did.

"Will you chop it off like this?" asked Jean, and he and Jeannette swung the ax. *Whack!* The ogress's head fell to the floor.

Jean and Jeannette carried her body to the bed, and balanced her head on top, and pulled up the cover. Then they hurried to the barn, and took the ogre's two horses, and hitched them to the ogre's golden carriage, and made their escape.

When the ogre came home and saw that there was no food on the table, he was as angry as a horsefly. "You useless heap of old bones!" he shouted at his wife. "How dare you loll about in bed while I am starving to death!" He grabbed the ogress by the hair, and—*whoosh!*—off came her head!

"Arrrrh!" the ogre cried. "What's going on here?" He ran to the stable, but his horses were gone. He ran to the barn, but his carriage was gone. He ran to the pigsty, but the boy was gone. The ogre knew at once what had happened. In a flash, he threw a saddle on his biggest pig, and began to ride furiously down the road.

By and by, the ogre came to a hunter, and shouted,

"Haven't you met
My Jean and Jeannette,
My horses so bold,
My carriage of gold?"

"What's that you say?" the hunter asked. "You want my dog to bark louder? Bark, Labri! Bark!"

"No," roared the ogre, "that's *not* what I said!" But Labri began to bark, and the ogre hurried off on his pig, howling with rage. Along the way he met a priest, and asked,

"Haven't you met
My Jean and Jeannette,
My horses so bold,
My carriage of gold?"

"What's that you say?" asked the priest. "Do you want me to ring the church bells louder?" And the priest rang the bells as loudly as he could.

"No," the ogre roared, "that's *not* what I said!" And off he galloped, with the poor pig underneath him grunting at the top of its lungs. Along the way he met three washerwomen by the side of a river. The ogre called out,

"Haven't you met
My Jean and Jeannette,
My horses so bold,
My carriage of gold?"

"Yes, we have," answered the washerwomen. "They rode by so quickly that the horses' hooves sent out sparks of lightning, and they crossed over to the other side of the river."

"But there isn't a bridge," said the ogre. "How can I get across?"

"Come here," said the washerwomen. "We will make a bridge from one of your hairs."

"Hurry up," said the ogre, and he lowered his head. The washerwomen pulled out one of his long hairs and threw it across the river. The ogre ran along the bridge of one hair, but when he got to the very middle, the bridge snapped, and he tumbled down into the water.

Then the ogre drowned, and the rooster crowed, and so my story is finished.

THE CAKE TREE

Sri Lanka

A man and a woman had seven sons. The six eldest worked in the rice fields, but the youngest, Sunil, was a small boy, and still in school. Every morning and every afternoon, he would walk with his friends to and from the schoolhouse in the next village. On their way they passed an old deserted house. But was it really deserted? No! A wicked raksasi—an ogress—had come to live there, along with her daughter, but no one in the village knew about them.

As the raksasi watched the children go by, she was overcome with a desire to catch them and eat them. One day, she arose before dawn, fried some sweet banana cakes, put them in a big sack, and carried them to a large tree that grew beside the road. She tied the cakes to the branches of the tree, and then she hid. Soon she heard the voices of the children.

"Look up there," one shouted.

"It's a cake tree!" cried another.

The boys and girls were so excited! They climbed the tree, and sat on the branches, and gobbled the banana cakes.

"This is no good at all," the raksasi complained. "There are too many of them. If I try to catch one or two, the rest will escape and tell their parents, and their parents will come after me. Wait! I think that tomorrow morning the greediest child will come earlier than the rest."

That night, Sunil lay awake thinking of nothing but the cake tree. He awoke and dressed before any of his schoolmates, and he left the village without them. He found the branches of the tree once again heavy with sweet banana cakes, and he quickly climbed up and began to eat.

The raksasi stepped out of the shadows. "Please throw down a cake for a hungry old woman," she whined. In the near-darkness, she looked like a woman from the village, and Sunil tossed down one of the cakes. The raksasi let it fall through her fingers.

"Oh, dear," she moaned. "There is dirt on that cake. I can't eat a dirty cake. Throw down another one, please, there's a nice fellow."

Sunil dropped another cake, but again the raksasi let it slip to the ground.

"I shall never catch one," the ogress whimpered. "I know what you should do. You should pick as many cakes as you can, and hold on to them, and jump down into my sack." She held out the sack and opened it wide.

The foolish child! He snatched as many cakes as he could from the tree, and clutching them tightly, he jumped. The raksasi caught him in her sack, hoisted the sack onto her shoulder, and ran home.

"Here is a tasty treat for us," she called to her daughter, and she dropped the sack on the floor. "Boil this little morsel right away while I wash myself in the river," she said.

The raksasi's daughter put a kettle of water on the fire. Then she opened the sack.

"Good morning, Auntie," said Sunil, smiling up at her.

The raksasi's daughter was puzzled. Was this boy in the sack her nephew? If he were, it wouldn't be right to cook him and eat him.

"Goodness gracious, Auntie!" cried Sunil, standing up. "I believe I see lice in your hair!"

"Please catch them for me, Nephew," the girl begged.

"Bend over this way and close your eyes, Auntie dear," said Sunil, and while her eyes were closed, he popped the sack onto the little raksasi and tied it tight. Then he seized a jar of oil from a shelf, and climbed a tall palm tree that stood by the raksasi's doorway. As he climbed, he tipped the jar so that oil oozed down the trunk of the tree.

Back from her bath, the raksasi sniffed the air eagerly. "Is breakfast ready, dear?" she asked as she entered the house. She saw the pot on the fire, but where was the boy? "You lazy girl!" she yelled. "Do I have to cook him myself?" She picked up the sack and emptied it into the pot, dumping her daughter into the boiling water. The girl screamed and tipped the pot and scrambled out. Just then, they heard Sunil's voice.

"Stupid cannibals! Raksasi!
You can't catch me! You can't catch me!"

The raksasi and her daughter ran out the door and looked up. There was Sunil at the top of the tree, grinning and making faces at them. They began to climb the tree, but the oil made them slip and crash to the ground. Soon they were blaming each other, and fighting, and pulling each other's hair. It was easy for Sunil to slip past them and run to the rice field. His father and mother and six brothers came with their hoes and sickles and chased the raksasi and her daughter out of the village forever.

THE RUNAWAY CHILDREN

South Africa: Xhosa

Long ago, in a time of famine, a woman named Nomagoda left her village and went to live in the forest, where she became a hunter. Nomagoda was so swift that no animal could outrun her. At first, she hunted game to feed herself and her son, Magoda. Then she began to hunt people as well. She became a cannibal.

The brother of Nomagoda remained in his village with his two young daughters. One day, he sent the girls to the river for water. One of the girls tripped on a rock, and fell, and broke the clay pot she was carrying. That pot was very valuable, and the girl was afraid to go back to her father, afraid that he would punish her.

"Let's run away to a place where our father won't be able to find us," said the girl to her sister. She was the younger and cleverer of the two, and so she was able to persuade her sister to follow her. The two of them went in the opposite direction from their home. For two days they walked. They were tired and hungry when at last they saw the smoke of a cooking fire in the distance. Following the smoke, they came to a house that stood all by itself in the woods.

At first, the girls were afraid to go in the house, but Magoda came out and talked to them, and they discovered that he was their cousin. "My mother, your aunt, is a cannibal," he said. "You should go away right now, before she comes home." Just then, they heard Nomagoda's footsteps, and the girls went into the house and hid.

Nomagoda appeared in the doorway. "I smell something nice," she said. "What is it, my son?"

"Nothing," he answered.

"Surely I smell fat children," said Nomagoda.

"No," said her son. "There are no children here."

"Don't I hunt for you?" Nomagoda scolded. "Don't I bring you animals to eat? Why are you hiding fat children from me?"

The girls couldn't help themselves. They cried out in fear, and Nomagoda rushed to their hiding place and grabbed them. "Why, you are my two nieces," she crooned. "Welcome to my house. Lie down, now, and go to sleep."

The girls lay down, but they were much too frightened to fall asleep. They could hear the sound of metal rubbing against stone as their aunt sang,

"Ax of mine, be sharp, be sharp.
Ax of mine, be sharp, be sharp."

"Oh!" the girls screamed.

"What's the matter with you two?" Nomagoda asked.

"Nothing," they answered. "Fleas are biting us."

"Get to sleep," said Nomagoda angrily, but she was becoming tired herself. She lay down beside them, and soon the girls heard her snoring. When Nomagoda snored, the ghosts of all the animals and all the people she had ever eaten moaned in her stomach and made an awful sound.

As soon as the girls were certain that their aunt was asleep, they crept out of bed, leaving two big stones in their place. They ran away as fast as they could.

Nomagoda awoke, and picked up her ax, and swung it at the two lumps next to her on the bed. *Clack, clang!* It fell on the hard stones.

Nomagoda screamed in rage. She ran outside and followed the children, smelling her way along the path they had taken. The cannibal did not travel like a person—she spun above the ground in the form of a whirlwind. From time to time, the girls looked behind them, and they saw the swirling cloud of dust that Nomagoda made as she ran. They could tell that she was getting closer and closer, and they knew they could not outrun her, so they climbed the tallest tree they could find and sat on a branch, staying still and quiet.

Nomagoda stopped in front of the tree and sniffed. "I know you are up there!" she shouted. She began to chop with her ax—*zukeke, zukeke, zukeke, zukeke.*

The tree was leaning over, about to fall, when a tiny intengu bird swooped down, singing,

"Intengu, intengu,
Chips, go back to your place.
I laugh with the tree,
Gomololo, gomololo,
The tree stands up again!"

The chips flew back into the tree trunk and stuck fast, and the tree stood straight and tall again. Nomagoda cursed and spat. She reached out and grabbed the intengu bird and stuffed it in her mouth and swallowed it, feathers and all. But as she did so, one small feather slipped out from between her lips and floated to the ground. Nomagoda did not see the feather fall. She began to chop at the tree again—*zukeke, zukeke, zukeke, zukeke.*

Then that one feather sang,

"Intengu, intengu,
Chips, go back to your place.
I laugh with the tree,
Gomololo, gomololo,
The tree stands up again!"

The chips flew back into the tree trunk and stuck fast, and the tree stood straight and tall again. Nomagoda cursed and spat. She reached out and grabbed the feather and swallowed it. Then she began to chop at the tree again—*zukeke, zukeke, zukeke, zukeke.*

She didn't notice, but a tiny little piece of meat flew out from between her teeth and fell on the ground. As Nomagoda chopped, the little piece of meat sang,

> "*Intengu, intengu,*
> Chips, go back to your place.
> I laugh with the tree,
> *Gomololo, gomololo,*
> The tree stands up again!"

The chips flew back into the tree trunk and stuck fast, and the tree stood straight and tall again. Nomagoda cursed and spat. She looked everywhere, but she couldn't find the piece of meat. It was just too small.

From their perch in the treetop, the girls could see a long way off. They saw two dogs as big as calves running toward them. The dogs looked like their father's dogs. Maybe their father was searching for them! The girls called them by name—*Mbam-bozo-lele! Ntum-ntum-she!*

The dogs came running to the tree and ate up the cannibal Nomagoda. All that remained were her bones. Her white bones lay on the ground beneath the tree.

The girls' father had been looking everywhere for his daughters. He was so glad to find them! He forgave them for breaking the pot and running away, and they all returned happily to their home.

NOTES

Tale type numbers for the following tales refer to the classification system developed by folklorists Antti Aarne and Stith Thompson, who analyzed and categorized thousands of tales from the oral tradition and arranged them into over 2,000 tale types. Each tale type has both a number and a descriptive name—for example, AT 510A, *Cinderella*. Tales that resemble a particular tale type are called variants—for example, the Irish tale "Fair, Brown, and Trembling" is a variant of AT 510A.

Aarne and Thompson designed their system for tales from a geographical area extending from India to Ireland, along with the lands settled by people from this area. Although quite a few tales from Africa and East Asia have counterparts in the Indo-European traditions, most are culture-specific, as are the tales of Polynesia, of Australia, and of the native peoples of the Americas. Each of these areas has its own typical tale themes and plots. Using methods similar to those of Aarne and Thompson, other scholars have created tale type indexes for different areas of the world.

The Three Little Piggies and Old Mister Fox / *United States: American-Scottish*

Joseph Jacobs's "The Story of Three Pigs," published in *English Fairy Tales* (1895), is the source of most modern versions of this tale. Jacobs adapted his version from J. O. Halliwells's *The Nursery Rhymes and Nursery Tales of England*, published forty years earlier. However, this American version differs in enough ways to identify it as an independent oral variant. The folktale collector, Mary Owen, transcribed it from a telling by Mrs. A. C. Ford, age eighty-two, in around 1900. Mrs. Ford heard this tale from her grandmother, who heard it from *her* grandmother, an immigrant from Scotland who arrived in Londonderry, New Hampshire, in 1718. In *Popular Tales of the West Highlands* (1860-62), John Francis Campbell reported that a similar story had been told in his Scottish family for at least three generations. The punctuation and typography are the work of the collector, and they convey an oral style perfectly suited to young listeners.

I was unable to locate any other folktale villains who were turned into butter. This motif is not listed in Stith Thompson's *Motif-Index of Folk*

Literature; however, students of children's literature will recognize this as the fate of the tigers in *Little Black Sambo* (1897). A butter churn is used for a different purpose in Jacobs's version—the third pig rolls home from the fair inside one to escape the wolf.

Tale type 124, *Blowing the House In*.

Big Pig, Little Pig, Speckled Pig, and Runt / *United States: African American*

This tale from Joel Chandler Harris's *Nights with Uncle Remus* is similar to several other nineteenth-century African American variants that appeared (in summary form) in *Lippincott's Magazine* and *Journal of American Folklore*. Harris begins his tale with five pigs, but the fifth, "Grunt," mysteriously disappears from the story before he can encounter Br'er Wolf, so I've left him out entirely. Other African American versions feature as many as seven pigs, which would make for a very long story.

Tale type 124, *Blowing the House In*.

The Three Geese / *Italy*

In most tales of this type from continental Europe, a group of farm animals take flight after they learn that they are about to be cooked for dinner. In this tale from Italy, however, it isn't clear why the three geese left home—only that they are alone and vulnerable. Unlike his counterpart in "The Three Pigs," who falls into a kettle of boiling water, the Italian wolf is tricked into drinking boiling water. This is a common episode in trickster tales around the world: the villain opens his mouth to eat the hero, and gets a mouthful of boiling water or oil instead.

Tale type 124, *Blowing the House In*.

How Jack Went to Seek His Fortune / *United States: Anglo-American*

Jack, the "everyboy" of British and American folktales, can do no wrong. Like his cousins—Hans in Germany, P'tit Jean in France, Juan Bobo in Latin America, and Ivan in Russia, to name a few—Jack always chances upon exactly the helpers he needs for the task or quest at hand. Some North American storytellers include a bee or a skunk among Jack's companions.

Tale type 130, *The Animals in Night Quarters*.

Medio Pollito / *Argentina*

The tale of the half chick has been extremely popular in the oral traditions of France, Spain, and Latin America. Storytellers explain the "half" in different ways. The chick might be literally half a chicken, split from top to bottom (and often transformed into a weathervane at the end of the tale), or he might be half the size a normal chick. In either case, he represents the unlikeliest of heroes, reminding the listener not to judge others' abilities by their size or appearance. In my retelling, I've followed the example of a minority of storytellers who relate that Medio Pollito's friends jumped into his beak. In most oral versions, the helpers hop into the other end of the chick's digestive tract.

Tale type 714, *Half Chick*.

Master Thumb / *Burma/Myanmar*

This tale is probably related to a myth about a culture hero who forced a sun god to send rain. Variants of this tale type, represented in the Grimms' collection by "Mister Korbes," have been recorded throughout Europe and Asia. Although this tale and the other two in this section have been assigned different tale type numbers, they are so similar that they should be recognized as part of a larger group that includes the Japanese "Momotaro" and the Chinese "Nung Gwama," among others.

Tale type 210, *Cock, Hen, Duck, Pin, and Needle on a Journey*.

Titeliture / *Sweden*

Tales of supernatural spinners are found throughout Europe, though they are rare elsewhere. A hapless girl might be ordered to spin straw into gold, as in this tale; or to spin a huge amount of flax, hemp, cotton, or wool in an impossibly short time; or to spin, weave, and sew a garment in a single night. When faced with such a task, who wouldn't hope for a magical helper? Yet in folk traditions a gift of help requires a gift in exchange, and the helper can name the price. On a metaphorical level, these tales convey the folk wisdom that there is a price to pay for accomplishing superhuman feats. They also reveal people's tendency to bargain with supernatural powers when in a difficult situation, and then to resist keeping their promise once the danger has passed.

In European tales, the name of the magical helper varies widely: Turandando in an Italian tale, Gwarwyn-a-throt in one from Wales, and Peerifool in a story from the Orkney Islands of Scotland, to name just a few.

Tale type 500, *The Name of the Helper*.

How Ijapa the Tortoise Tricked the Hippopotamus / *Nigeria: Yoruba*

African and African American tales about secret names follow different patterns from European ones. In some, a king will wed his daughters only to men who can guess their secret names. In others, the fruits of a magic tree can be eaten only by those who know the tree's secret name.

The tortoise is a slow, conniving trickster in African folktales. Although he is small and weak, he can outwit even the spider and the hare. Eight uppity hippopotamuses are no match for him. Ijapa the tortoise is the hero of a great many Yoruba trickster tales.

Oniroku / *Japan*

In some Japanese folktales, oni are the equivalent of European child-stealing ogres. In other tales, like this one, oni are powerful creatures of forest, river, and mountain who may either harm or help human beings. This Japanese tale resembles several northern European legends of trolls who help humans construct bridges and churches. According to wide-spread folk belief, a building cannot stand and endure unless the spirits of the place have given their permission. "Oniroku" features a nature spirit who not only consents to the building of the bridge, he performs all the work as well.

Princess Tombi-ende and the Frog / *Swaziland*

Frogs are associated with survival and rebirth in the myths and tales of southern Africa. These beliefs are inspired by the behavior of real frogs that bury themselves in the mud and sleep during the dry season, then re-emerge when the rains begin. Gathering red clay was a female occupation in Africa. Many folktales of girls' adventures begin with a journey to a clay pit located far from their village.

How a Warty Toad Became an Emperor / *China: Hmong*

Like Tombi-ende's frog, this enchanted toad passes difficult tests and performs superhuman feats in order to win the bride who will help him become human. Nai-tung Ting lists forty-two versions of this tale in his *Type Index of Chinese Folktales*. In one, a princess tosses a brocaded ball to her suitors and the one who catches it wins her hand in marriage. A lowly frog succeeds—reminding the reader of the Grimms' frog retrieving the princess's golden ball.

Tale type 440, *The Frog King or Iron Henry.*

Little Singing Frog / *Serbia*

Most tales of the frog or mouse princess are told from the male protagonist's point of view: A king has promised his throne to whichever of his three sons finds the most skillful bride. The three princes leave home in search of young women who excel at traditional female tasks, such as weaving and baking. The youngest prince brings home a small animal and is ridiculed, but his animal bride wins the competition and is transformed into a lovely young woman. When this tale is told from the female protagonist's point of view, as in "Little Singing Frog," it becomes a Cinderella story, except that the heroine succeeds through skill and knowledge rather than through kindness and beauty.

Tale type 402, *The Mouse (Cat, Frog, etc.) as Bride.*

Jean and Jeannette / *France*

The word "ogre" comes from Latin *Orcus*, the name of an ancient god of death (sometimes associated with the Roman god Pluto) who was believed to capture the living and carry them to the underworld. The ogre is the star bogeyman of French children's stories. In folktales, humans can enter the realm of magic, but most creatures of that world, scary ones in particular, are excluded from ours—in the case of the ogre in "Jean and Jeannette," by a bridge of one hair. Traveling on a bridge of one hair is an old storytelling motif found in tales of King Arthur, in Norse myth, and in Islamic religious tradition.

Tale type 327 A, *Hansel and Gretel.*

The Cake Tree / *Sri Lanka*

According to *The Ramayana,* the ancient epic of India, Raksasi and Raksasa were created by the god Brahma as guardians of the waters. In folktales, these creatures play the familiar role of the stupid ogre. Sri Lankan raksasas are child-stealers. They have green-blue skin, matted hair, and huge bellies. Their eyes are vertical slits, and their tongues are two or three times longer than human tongues. This is the raksasa in its ugliest form, and it's important to note that they are shape-changers and can look just like ordinary people when they choose, except for the one feature they can't change—their fingers are attached backward to their hands. Calling a raksasa "Auntie" is a foolproof way to buy the time to escape. It will take the dimwitted monster a long time to decide whether a child is her niece (or nephew), in which case it would be taboo to eat them.

Tale type 327 C, *The Devil (Witch) Carries the Hero Home in a Sack.*

The Runaway Children / *South Africa: Xhosa*

Because few African folktales conform to the Aarne-Thompson tale types, folklorists have created other classification systems for Africa as a whole, and for specific cultural areas within Africa. William Bascom identified nine major African tale plots not found in Europe, including *Dogs Rescue Master from Tree Refuge*. "The Runaway Children" belongs to this group, as do the African American tales "Barney McCabe" and "Wiley and the Hairy Man." The intengu, also known as the fork-tail drongo, or bee-catcher, is a real bird thought to have magical powers.

WORKS CONSULTED

Aarne, Antti, and Stith Thompson. *The Types of the Folktale: A Classification and Bibliography.* 2nd revision. Helsinki: Suomalainen Tiedeakatemia, 1961.

Bascom, William R. *African Folktales in the New World.* Bloomington: Indiana University Press, 1992.

Campbell, John Francis. *Popular Tales of the West Highlands.* 4 vols. Edinburgh: Edmonston and Douglas, 1860-62.

Crane, Thomas Frederick. *Italian Popular Tales.* Boston: Houghton Mifflin, 1885.

Dayrell, Elphinstone. *Folk Stories from Southern Nigeria, West Africa.* London: Longmans, Green, and Co., 1910.

Delarue, Paul. *The Borzoi Book of French Folk Tales.* New York: Knopf, 1956.

Eberhard, Wolfram. *Typen Chinesischer Volksmärchen.* Helsinki: Suomalainen Tiedeakatemia, 1937.

Fillmore, Parker. *The Laughing Prince.* New York: Harcourt, Brace and Company, 1921.

Folk Tales from China. 3rd series. Peking Foreign Languages Press, 1958.

Graham, David Crockett. *Songs and Stories of the Ch'uan Miao.* Washington, D.C.: Smithsonian Institution, 1954.

Harris, Joel Chandler. *Nights with Uncle Remus.* Boston: Houghton Mifflin, 1883.

Htin Aung, Maung. *Burmese Folk-Tales.* Calcutta: Oxford University Press, 1948.

Massignon, Geneviève. *De bouche à oreilles: Le conte populaire en France.* Paris Berger-Levrault, 1983.

——. *Folktales of France.* Translated by Jacqueline Hyland. Chicago: University of Chicago Press, 1968.

Owen, Mary A. "The Three Pigs." *Journal of American Folklore* 15 (1902).

Owomoyela, Oyekan. *Yoruba Trickster Tales.* Lincoln: University of Nebraska Press, 1997.

Parker, H. Langloh. *Village Tales of Ceylon.* Vol. 1. Dehiwala, Sri Lanka: Tisafa Prakasakayo, 1910.

Scheub, Harold. *The Xhosa Ntsomi.* Oxford: Clarendon Press, 1975.

Sébillot, Paul. *Littérature orale de l'Auvergne.* Paris: J. Maisonneuve, 1898.

Theal, George McCall. *Kaffir Folk-Lore.* London: S. Schonnenschein, Le Bas & Lowrey, 1882.

Thompson, Stith. *Motif-Index of Folk Literature: A Classification of Narrative Elements in Folk-Tales, Ballads, Myths, Fables, and Medieval Romances.* Bloomington: Indiana University Press, 1932-36.

Thompson, Stith, and Warren E. Roberts. *Types of Indic Oral Tales: India, Pakistan, and Ceylon.* Helsinki: Suomalainen Tiedeakatemia, 1960.

——. *The Folktale.* Berkeley: University of California Press, 1977, c1946.

Ting, Nai-tung. *A Type Index of Chinese Folktales in the Oral Tradition and Major Works of Non-Religious Classical Literature.* Helsinki: Suomalainen Tiedeakatemia, 1978.

Vidal de Battini, Berta E. *Cuentos y Leyendas Populares de la Argentina.* Vol. 2. Buenos Aires: Ediciones Culturales Argentinas, 1980.

Werner, Alice. *Myths and Legends of the Bantu.* London: G. G. Harrap, 1933.

Zenani, Nongenile Masithathu. *The World and the Word: Tales and Observations from the Xhosa Oral Tradition.* Madison: University of Wisconsin Press, 1992.